# Let's Read

# The Toy Cupboard

Jane Fior   Pictures by Gill Chapman

COLLINS COLOUR CUBS

I like to play in the garden,
but when it rains
we have to stay indoors.

"Go upstairs," Mum says.
"See what you can find
in the toy cupboard."

First of all, I take out
a big cardboard box
and set up my trains.

Teddy wants a ride.
The toys have to watch.
There's no room for them!

Jenny has a truck with bricks.
She likes to push it round the room.

I'm going to build a station
for my trains.
I'll build a garage too,
with petrol pumps.

The cars can go in the car park.

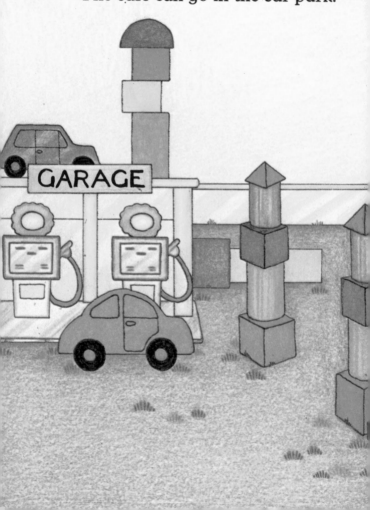

This car is a taxi. It collects Teddy from the station, and takes him over to the dolls' house.

The dolls' house has four rooms;
a kitchen, a living room, a bedroom,
and a bathroom. Six dolls
live in the dolls' house.

They are going to have a tea-party.
The tea-set is in the toy cupboard.

I'll pour the tea.
It's too difficult for the dolls.

I think the dolls would like to go
to the country for a treat.
Here comes the red bus.

First of all, the bus stops
at the farm. The sheep look
over the hedge. They are very surprised
to see the dolls.

The farmer's wife is feeding the hens.
The farmer's dog sits in his kennel.
He looks fierce but he does not bark.

Quick, dolls! Back in the bus.
We are going to the zoo.

I must build cages for the animals.
I'll make them nice and big
and put lots of trees around.

The dolls like the zoo.
They want to stay and look at all
the animals. But they have to get back
in the bus. It's time to go home.

Oh dear! Matilda has fallen out
of the bus. I think
she has broken her leg.

Doctor, doctor, come quickly!
Matilda has broken her leg.

Here is the doctor with his doctor's bag.
Matilda has to have a bandage.
Matilda has to go to bed.

Teddy will look after Matilda.
He will bring her drinks of water
and read her stories.

The doctor drives to the station
in his fast car.
He is just in time to catch the train.

The train has to go through the tunnel.
It is *very* dark and noisy.
The toys in the train are frightened.
They are pleased to get out of the train
and back into . . .

ISBN 0 00 196037 7
Text and illustrations © William Collins Sons & Co Ltd 1981
Printed in Great Britain

the toy cupboard.